# LESBIAN/ SAPPHIC ROMANCE 2

*Age Gap Ice Queen CEO Romance*

**Maureen Lester**

# TABLE OF CONTENTS

# Chapter One

## The Heart Attack

23-year-old Elizabeth Peterson had worked as Mrs. Madison's personal assistant for just short of a month, but she was by far the best thing that had ever happened to the 55-year-old businesswoman. It had taken a little convincing, but Mrs. Madison had now trained her to be a 'full-service PA' as Mrs. Madison liked to call it. Whenever the horny old businesswoman was stressed, her stacked assistant was always willing to provide manual, oral, or even vaginal stress relief.

The stunning blonde woman was fully naked and hunched over the edge of Mrs. Madison's desk at that precise moment.

Mrs. Madison, the personal assistant's employer, was standing behind the sexy personal assistant as her short gray skirt and pink g-string underwear were crumpled in a heap on the opposite side of the office. Her boss' hands were firmly gripping the blonde's slender hips as she fucked her, and the strap-on cock was buried to the hilt in her delectably tight snatch.

"That's it Elizabeth, take my cock!" grunted Mrs. Madison as she humped against her gorgeous assistant's posterior. Each hard thrust of her pelvis caused her hips to slap loudly against Elizabeth's lovely round ass and the cock to plunge deep inside her tight, clutching pussy. Having ready access to the rather gullible young blonde's delightful orifices was a dream come true for old Mrs. Madison.

Mrs. Madison thought Elizabeth was the most gorgeous woman she had ever seen. She almost made her boss drool when she stared at her for too long due to her long, peroxide-blonde hair, huge breasts, and toned, hourglass figure. She was also really stupid and naive on top of all that. The ideal formula for Mrs. Madison's sleazy deceptions.

At first, her stress relief duties had been rather minor; Mrs. Madison simply substituted her trusty old thinking putty for Elizabeth's magnificent round breasts. But with a few clever lies and manipulations, things quickly escalated to handjobs, then poon jobs, and eventually full sex. Not to mention milking her boss' tits as well. These days, Elizabeth spent more time sucking and fucking than she did typing and filing.

Elizabeth groaned as her boss violently slammed the stiff prick into her, pushing her curvy body up against the desk. Her boss was under a lot of stress today.

As Mrs. Madison's thrusts became more and

more frantic, Elizabeth wondered if her boss would pull out and replace the cock with Elizabeth's mouth and have her swallow her pussy juices, as she jammed Elizabeth's face into her pussy. Or if she'd squirt into Elizabeth's pussy today, after crushing their cunts together, tribbing her with reckless abandon.

At Mrs. Madison's suggestion, they'd been trying to cut back on the milking and poon jobs, Elizabeth's husband had been complaining about her breath recently, but despite her best efforts, Elizabeth regularly found her mouth on her boss' pussy or tits.

"Oh, fuck yeah!" grunted Elizabeth, her boss pistoning the cock in and out of her cunt.

Mrs. Madison gave a sudden gasp and Elizabeth felt her tense, her rapid thrusting suddenly halting, the cock buried deep inside her.

She gave a small strangled grunt and then there was a strange gasp and Elizabeth suddenly felt the crushing weight of her boss slumping down on top of her back, pinning her to the desk.

"Mrs. Madison?" she asked uncertainly.

There was no reply. Mrs. Madison's cock was still buried in Elizabeth's twat. "Are you okay, Mrs. Madison?"

"Call..." gasped Mrs. Madison, her voice sounding exceedingly strained, "9...1...1..." With that she gave a strange gurgle and passed out.

## Chapter Two

### Day One

The next morning Elizabeth arrived at work feeling rather guilty.

It turned out that Mrs. Madison hadn't died, as Elizabeth had initially feared after squirming out from underneath her, but she had suffered a fairly bad heart attack. Elizabeth had called an ambulance and then quickly got dressed again before it arrived. Naturally, she had to put away Mrs. Madison's strap-on cock and refasten her pants.

She'd been called by head office that morning and told Mrs. Madison was expected to be in hospital for at least three weeks and that a trusted member of the senior management team, a Mrs. Smith would come to look after things while she was recuperating.

Elizabeth, of course, felt horrible about the whole situation. It wasn't the fact that Mrs. Madison had suffered her attack while she was fucking her, but more that she was not doing a very good job relieving the poor woman's stress. For her to have such a bad heart attack meant that she was still stressed, despite Elizabeth's best efforts. She had to admit to herself that on some occasions, usually when Mrs. Madison called on her several times in one day and her pussy or jaw was particularly sore or tired, she hadn't truly put her heart into her duties. She promised herself that she'd do a lot better if she got another chance.

The busty blonde secretary arrived nice and early to make sure that everything would be ready for her new though temporary boss. She gave the office a quick tidy and ensured that all her filing was up to date so that she could divert her full attention to whatever duties the new boss would give her. With all the tit-sucking and pussy eating she'd been doing over the past few weeks she was a little behind on her filing.

At about 10 am Mrs. Smith; Elizabeth's new boss, arrived.

Mrs. Smith was a lot younger than Elizabeth had expected, she looked to be in her early forties, quite a change after having 55-year-old Esther Madison.

She was dressed in a very smart three-piece suit.

"You must be Mrs. Smith," said Elizabeth as her new boss entered the office. "I'm Elizabeth Peterson, Mrs. Madison's personal assistant."

"G...Elizabeth, good morning," I stumbled as I extended my hand to the attractive young lady. The stunningly seductive blonde who was there to greet me caught me off guard.

But as I began to become wet, I began to wonder what it would feel like to lick a woman's pussy, especially Elizabeth's pussy. I've never desired to lick another woman's lips or her breasts. I've never been with a woman before.

I was in my mid-forties, forty-four to be precise, and happily married. I think I am fairly attractive, red hair, and green eyes and I was pretty trim for my age; I've recognized the 'look' from men in public that said I looked pretty hot so felt pretty confident in my looks.

To impress her new boss, Elizabeth had dressed to the nines. She was dressed in a black silk top that clung to her stunning contours and was stretched taut across her ample bosom and tapered into her waist. She was wearing a short, matching black skirt that fit almost like a second skin over her hips, thighs, and cherry ass. She was accessorizing her long, slender legs with tall high heels and beautiful black tights below the skirt. I found it quite difficult to take my eyes off Elizabeth because she had such a hot, though professional look.

"Mrs. Madison's...er, I mean your office is right this way," said Elizabeth as she led me to my new office.

The sight of the curvaceous blonde had destroyed my composure, and as I followed her to my office, I couldn't help but ogle her lovely round ass, swaying seductively inside her short skirt as she went. What was wrong with me?

Elizabeth turned to face me once more, and I struggled to keep my composure and pull my sight away from the massive globes of her chest. "Yes. I'm grateful to you, Elizabeth. I'll be with you soon to go through how things will go for the next few weeks until Mrs. Madison is healthy enough to return, so please give me a moment to settle in. It was terrible to learn of her heart attack."

Elizabeth blushed, unable to ignore the guilt she was feeling. "Yes, terrible news," she agreed.

With that Mrs. Smith gave a curt nod and shut the office door, leaving a slightly surprised Elizabeth to return to her desk in the reception area.

"Fucking hell she's gorgeous," I muttered under my breath, playing with my pussy, imagining it was her hand playing with my clit. I couldn't be certain, but I was pretty sure I'd seen the slight jut of her nipples through her silk blouse. Was she wearing a bra? The combined thought of sucking her hard nipples with her hand on my wet pussy was so erotic that I soon brought myself to orgasm.

Like I said I'd never been with a woman before so I found my reaction to Elizabeth surprising.

But I had work to do and got on with it as best I could.

## Chapter Three

### Elizabeth Is Baffled

It wasn't until almost 4 o'clock that Mrs. Smith emerged from behind the closed door of her office to speak with Elizabeth. The very first thing that Elizabeth noticed was that in Mrs. Smith's left hand was a rather familiar-looking blue thinking putty.

Elizabeth frowned slightly at the sight of Mrs. Madison's old thinking putty. "Ah, where did you find that?" she asked.

Mrs. Smith frowned, looking down at the ball almost as if she'd forgotten she'd been holding it. She squeezed it. "Oh, this? It was in Esther's top drawer. I kind of like it, it's soothing."

"Oh, I see," croaked Elizabeth. She was sure that Mrs. Madison had said she'd lost that thing. On the plus side, it meant that she'd be saved from the embarrassment of Mrs. Smith using her boobs instead. Elizabeth had always felt a little awkward when Mrs. Madison had used them as a replacement for the thinking putty.

"Anyway," continued Mrs. Smith. "I know it's getting late but I thought we'd better discuss how things work around here. What are your usual duties?"

Elizabeth blushed. She wasn't quite sure how much she should tell Mrs. Smith. Mrs. Madison's demands were perhaps a little...unusual. "Um, mostly filing and typing. And a little dictation. Anything you need really," she eventually replied.

Mrs. Smith nodded. "Very good. And is there anything scheduled for tomorrow I need to be aware of?"

Elizabeth thought for a moment. "Um, Mrs. Madison usually takes a conference call on

Wednesday mornings."

Mrs. Smith frowned. "Really? I'm not aware of any conference calls. Oh well, never mind, we can sort that out tomorrow. I need to head home so I'll see you in the morning."

She grabbed a breath mint from the small bowl on the edge of Elizabeth's desk and popped it in her mouth.

"Goodnight Mrs. Smith," said Elizabeth as her new boss left the office. It felt kind of strange to be finished for the day. Her first day without Mrs. Madison. It almost felt like she hadn't done any work today, despite all the filing she'd put away that morning. She hadn't once licked or rubbed or even seen a pussy the entire day. It just felt... peculiar.

# Chapter Four

## The Next Morning

The next morning Elizabeth once again arrived looking her best. She was more determined than ever to make a good impression on her new boss after their somewhat awkward first day together. She was wearing a tight-fitting white top that accentuated the impressive thrust of her sizable bust and a short beige skirt that was slit up one side displaying a good expanse of her tanned thigh. Although Mrs. Madison obviously wouldn't be around to play with her tits, she still wore no bra out of habit, and her hard nipples were discernible through the thin material of her top.

Once again I was stopped in my tracks at the sight of her. "Um, Elizabeth..." I eventually managed to squeak as I tore my eyes away from her chest.

"Yes, Mrs. Smith?"

"It may be embarrassing, but I must inquire: are you wearing a brassiere," I asked with a little bit of a stutter.

With a startled sigh, she unconsciously cupped her hands over her protruding breasts to hide her nipple points. "Oh. I'm not, no. Mrs. Madison advised against wearing one."

I thought to myself, Did she now? Interesting...

Elizabeth blushed at her admission and wondered if perhaps it was a mistake to tell her new boss about Mrs. Madison's request.

As I watched Elizabeth's hands cup her breasts through the fitted white top she was wearing, I couldn't help but notice how small her hands appeared in comparison to the size of her bosom, or perhaps I should say how large they appeared...

"If you think it's unprofessional, I'd be happy to wear a bra to work from now on, if you want, Mrs. Smith."

That was the last thing I wanted. What I wanted was for her to fuck my face with her tits.

"Well if Mrs. Madison in her wisdom saw no reason for you to wear a bra, who am I to complain," I managed to say at last. "Um... Carry on."

With that I hurried to my office and shut the door, leaving Elizabeth alone in the reception area once again.

Elizabeth took a deep breath and dropped her hands away from her chest. Things were not going well with Mrs. Smith, she decided in discomfort. She was very different from Mrs. Madison. There was an awkwardness or tension between the two of them and she wasn't sure what to do about it.

The beautiful young personal assistant shook her head and returned to her desk. As she sat down she realized that she didn't have any work to do. In all honesty, most of her job involved helping Mrs. Madison remain calm and stress-free. Mrs. Smith didn't seem to require her in that capacity and so she seemed to have a lot of free time on her hands.

Elizabeth sighed again and reached into her top drawer for her nail file. It was going to be a long day.

It took a good hour to get her nails perfected and then Elizabeth decided she should probably actually do some work. Of course, she didn't have anything that needed doing, this business of having a self-sufficient boss made her a little nervous about her job.

Would Mrs. Smith fire her if she wasn't needed anymore? Surely she'd have to wait for Mrs. Madison to return first?

Elizabeth stood up and walked over to the filing cabinet, deciding that she should probably check to make sure the filing she did yesterday was done correctly. It wouldn't look good if Mrs. Smith found any mistakes in her work.

As she pulled open the drawer and bent at the waist to check the alphabetization of the files Mrs. Smith opened her office door.

I licked my lips and swallowed at the sight that greeted me. Bent at the waist with her back to me, Elizabeth's flawless round ass was thrust straight at me. Her round, peachy buttocks were presented, her short beige skirt pulled taut across them, and her legs appeared even longer and sexier from the back.

Staring intently at my PA's gloriously firm-looking ass, I was sooo tempted to grab or hump those magnificent buttocks, but of course, that would be completely unprofessional, not to mention illegal and against the company's sexual harassment policy.

Eventually, I snapped out of my daze and got Elizabeth's attention by clearing my throat.

"Oh, I didn't see you there Mrs. Smith," said Elizabeth as she straightened up and turned to face me.

"Ah yes. I just wondered if you had some time to do some dictation and typing for me."

"Of course," agreed Elizabeth earnestly, pleased that Mrs. Smith finally needed her for something. "I'll just grab my pad and pen."

We both moved back to my office, Elizabeth pulling up a chair so that she was sitting right beside me as I dictated a business letter to her.

Having her sit so close to me made me rather excited, and I couldn't help but admire her nicely tanned and perfectly toned thighs as she crossed her long legs, her short skirt riding up even higher on her smooth thighs. I badly wanted to duck my head between those thighs.

As I made my way through the letter, I frequently shifted uncomfortably in my chair and the whole process took about twice as long as it should have.

At one point Elizabeth uncrossed and re-crossed her long, sexy legs, causing me to cream my panties even more.

As Elizabeth sat next to Mrs. Smith, diligently writing down every word she said, she glanced down out of the corner of her eye at her boss' lap. To her surprise her boss' right hand was on her crotch, surreptitiously rubbing her pussy through her suit pants.

Elizabeth bit her lip and held her breath a moment as she tried to decide what she should do. If it had been Mrs. Madison, she would have immediately offered to relieve her. Actually, if she'd been Mrs. Madison, she would probably already have shoved Elizabeth's pretty little mouth on her naked pussy, but she wasn't sure what Mrs. Smith would want.

Would she be offended if she offered her a poon job or maybe even a quick handjob? Elizabeth didn't want to do the wrong thing here and get herself fired. But surely, as Mrs. Madison had told her on numerous occasions, it was her job to relieve her boss's stress. Right?

Mrs. Smith suddenly crossed her legs, removing her hand from her crotch. Elizabeth glanced up at her face and saw her looking at her, her eyes very green. She'd caught her staring at her crotch! Elizabeth swallowed in embarrassment and hurriedly returned her attention to her notes.

"Okay, that's it," I said, finishing the letter. "Can you type that up before the end of the day please?"

"Yes, Mrs. Smith," replied Elizabeth obediently. She hesitated a moment, still undecided on whether she should offer to help her new boss deal with her uncomfortable situation. "Um... Mrs. Smith?"

"Yes, Elizabeth?"

"Would you..." she paused for a moment, glancing down at my crotch. "Would you like me to..."

"Why did Mrs. Madison ask you not to wear a bra?"

My question seemed to catch her by surprise.

Hesitantly, Elizabeth responded, "Well, Mrs. Madison needed stress relief since she had misplaced her thinking putty."

I considered how intriguing this was becoming.

"And how did you make this relief possible?"

Elizabeth blurted out while blushing, "Um, squeezing my breasts appeared to help at first then -"

I creamed myself some more. But this needed careful going.

"Perhaps, I would be needing some stress relief soon myself. For now, I need to get back to work Elizabeth," I hurriedly cut in, interrupting her.

"Sorry, I'll get onto this letter," Elizabeth quickly replied before standing up to leave, her courage rapidly deserting her. Had she guessed what she was going to say? Did she not want her help? Things were so confusing for the busty young PA. At least with Mrs. Madison, she'd been left with no doubt in what she wanted from her.

Her mind still filled with doubts and questions, Elizabeth hurriedly left Mrs. Smith's office and returned to her desk. In a few weeks, Mrs. Madison would be back and things would return to normal.

For most of the rest of the day, Mrs. Smith did her best to avoid Elizabeth, pretty much locking herself in her office the entire afternoon.

Elizabeth was still very unsure of herself and her future but resolved to make a bigger effort to impress Mrs. Smith to ensure her job was safe.

Even though she had hardly any work on, Elizabeth made sure she stayed later than Mrs. Smith, just so that she looked good.

It was almost 6:30 when Mrs. Smith finally emerged from his office.

"Oh, Elizabeth? You're still here," I remarked a little startled, "I assumed you'd be long gone by now."

"Just finishing a few things up Mrs. Smith," replied Elizabeth, feeling rather pleased with herself for staying late and giving the appearance of being hard-working.

"Well, I'll see you in the morning," said Mrs. Smith, heading for the door.

"Good job today Mrs. Smith," said Elizabeth, reaching out and lightly patting her boss's bottom as she walked past.

Mrs. Smith froze at the touch of her hand on her ass.

At her reaction, Elizabeth's heart lurched. Had she stuffed things up again? She was just trying to remember the things that Mrs. Madison had taught her. "Just a pat for a job well done...since we are teammates, right?" she added lamely.

"Yes, we are Elizabeth," I said slowly turning round. "Is this another one of the things Mrs. Smith asked of you?"

"Um, yes. But if it makes you uncomfortable..."

"No, not at all. Since we are teammates, it's only natural I reciprocate the gesture, right?"

To my surprise, she happily conceded.

"Of course, you can," replied Elizabeth, inwardly she was jumping for joy, very pleased that Mrs. Smith was happy with her.

She turned around and bent over slightly, pushing her nicely rounded ass out towards her boss. Her perfect posterior was displayed when the black dress' material strained taut across it.

I swallowed and licked my lips as I slowly, almost reached out and placed my hand on Elizabeth's firm ass. God, I wanted to hump her so bad I could barely see straight.

It wasn't a pat, I just left my hand there, cupping the round globe of Elizabeth's left buttock.

Elizabeth glanced over her shoulder at her boss, but she was staring down at her ass as if it was the most amazing thing she'd ever laid eyes upon.

It took all my will not to rub my wet pussy against her ass.

My hand still wasn't patting. It was merely holding Elizabeth's buttock, not even squeezing or stroking the firm globe.

Elizabeth was also frozen, she was not sure what to do. Her boss wasn't patting her the way she'd expected, or even copping a feel like Mrs. Madison tended to do. "Are you okay Mrs. Smith?" she asked cautiously.

"I am very okay, Elizabeth," I said in a voice I hardly recognized. "Bend over the desk."

Elizabeth was a little surprised by the tone of her boss' voice. It sounded like the purr of a feline.

She seemed to be making a big deal out of what was supposed to be a quick pat on the butt, but she leaned forward, bending over the edge of the desk and presenting her ass towards her boss.

"Wow," I breathed in awe as I placed both

my hands on Elizabeth's flawless ass, taking a firm buttock in each palm. My clit screamed in agony for relief as it throbbed.

I gave the round globes a slight squeeze, amazed at their firmness. "Beautiful," I murmured as my right hand began to rub Elizabeth's right buttock, my palm stroking her ass in small circles, almost worshiping her gorgeous ass.

Elizabeth couldn't help but feel good at the obvious admiration her boss seemed to have for her ass. She'd always considered her ample breasts to be her best feature. Perhaps squeezing her ass helped Mrs. Smith relax, much like Mrs. Madison using her hooters as thinking putty.

"Oh, yes..." I groaned as I rubbed Elizabeth's buttock.

Mrs. Smith was certainly sounding pretty happy, thought Elizabeth.

My hand slid down over her hip, along the outside of her thigh, down past the hem of her skirt. "Fuck," I muttered under my breath as I slid my hand back up her stocking-clad thigh, slipping up inside the slit on the side of her skirt to touch, past the lace top of her stocking, to the exposed skin of her upper thigh.

I froze for a moment, my hand up beneath the hem of her skirt. "Stop," I said aloud. "We need to stop."

I quickly withdrew my hand. "Yes. Excellent work, Elizabeth." Then made a brisk exit from the office without turning around.

Elizabeth was disappointed that she seemed to have once again upset her strange new boss.

She was kicking herself as she went back to her desk. She should have tried to figure out a way to give Mrs. Smith a poon job.

It had worked with Mrs. Madison, helping her to relieve stress; if she could get her mouth on Mrs. Smith's pussy, she'd win her over for sure. She probably should have just come out and offered to lick her pussy, but with Mrs. Smith's current strange mood, no doubt she would have turned her down.

The slender blonde sighed and returned to her chair.

She had to come up with a plan or a trick to get Mrs. Smith's clit into her mouth, she would never agree if she just straight out offered her oral.

Elizabeth picked up a pen off her desk and tapped it against her chin as she tried to remember back to a few weeks ago when she'd first licked Mrs. Madison's pussy. It had been for stress relief reasons, right? No, that was later, the first time was when she'd had to clean her up after spilling coffee on her and she ended up giving her boss a handjob. Another day she milked her boss by sucking her tits because she didn't want to use breast pumps anymore. Probably found it an unhygienic practice because of the baby. By the way, wasn't he too old to still be breastfeeding?

She'd ended up licking her boss' clit and swallowing her pussy juices to stop from making a mess of the office.

Surely after the job-well-done pat she received from Mrs. Smith today, she should be able to come up with something to progress to relieving herself on her ass.

Of course, first, she had to get her boss to rub herself on her ass...

## Chapter Five

## The Next Level

After finally groping the sweet ass of my assistant, Elizabeth - which had been part of my fantasy since I first assumed work as her boss - I was still visions of her deep blue eyes staring up at me, her tongue lapping moistly over my pussy lips, and her magnificent pussy covering my face as I delighted in licking her bombarded my mind. As I prepared and had the typical evening meal with my spouse, these pictures kept running through my head.

"You seem a little keyed up," noted Sam as he helped me with the dishes.

"Yeah. A lot is happening at work, " I whispered.

Fortunately, he was exhausted and preferred sleeping over having sex, giving me time in bed to reflect on the day. I was unsure whether or not Sam would view my having sex with another lady as having an affair since I had never left our marriage. Additionally, I was concerned about working with Elizabeth because I was afraid that I wouldn't be able to control my impulses around her. I couldn't afford to lose the job because I was too preoccupied with thoughts of eating Elizabeth's pussy to concentrate on my duties.

God help me, I was married, but I wanted Elizabeth. I wanted to kiss and lick her slit while feeling my wet face slide over her pussy. I wanted to look down to see her beautiful face between my legs with her hot wet tongue slithering noisily in and out of my cunt and over my pussy lips.

I had trouble sleeping the entire night, but I knew I had to go to the workplace the following morning since I had tasks to complete and couldn't allow my mind to wander.

That next morning, Elizabeth arrived at work feeling more confident than ever. She knew exactly how she was going to get herself back into her new boss's good graces and prove her worth.

The gorgeous blonde was today wearing a black, slightly flared, and loose-fitting skirt that was quite short, displaying a good portion of her smooth thighs, and an even more impressive portion when it flared out as she walked around the office, rising up around her long legs. She'd chosen not to wear stockings today, to allow Mrs. Smith access to her smooth legs in case she wanted to touch them.

The skirt was matched to a tight-fitting, white long-sleeved top that had a plunging v-neckline that displayed plenty of her deep cleavage. Of course, she wore no bra beneath.

As Elizabeth moved around behind Mrs. Smith's desk to pour her morning coffee, she bent slightly at the waist and thrust out her round, perky posterior, most invitingly. Elizabeth realized that when it came to Rachael. Smith, her best asset was her world-class bum.

"Good job Elizabeth," said Mrs. Smith, Elizabeth's tactic paying off. Her hand boldly slid up the back of her smooth thigh to cup her ass beneath her skirt.

Elizabeth had been careful not to wear any panties today, and when Mrs. Smith's hand reached her ass it was filled with the silky, uncovered curve of her right buttock.

I moaned as I squeezed the warm, soft flesh.

"I've checked your diary, and Mr. Collins

from head office is coming in at 10 am," explained Elizabeth, straightening up. Mrs. Smith's left hand remained up her skirt, attached to her ass, but Elizabeth acted as though it wasn't there.

"Yes, I must make a good impression," I purred, picking up my coffee cup with one hand as my other hand caressed my assistant's ass.

"If there's anything at all I can do to help, let me know," said Elizabeth and smiled broadly.

"Thank you Elizabeth," I replied, patting her bare buttock. I let my hand drop down from beneath her short skirt, my palm running down the back of her smooth thigh before falling away. "I had better prepare my reports for Mr. Collins."

"Of course," nodded Elizabeth. "Remember. If there is anything at all I can do. Simply call me on the intercom."

With that, Elizabeth made for the door, feeling rather pleased with herself, making sure to sway her sensational ass as she walked.

Just before she reached the office door she dropped her pen and bent over slowly, so slowly to retrieve it. I saw her bare ass, as her skirt rode up.

She stood and turned toward me.

"I must be nervous today," she said and she smiled at me and turned again, and left the office.

It was clear the display was intentional on her part. As soon as she left, I played with my pussy, again imagining it was her hand playing with my clit but before I could bring myself to orgasm, the office door suddenly opened and there Elizabeth stood looking startled.

"Oh my goodness, Mrs. Smith?" blurted out Elizabeth in apparent surprise. Something in me snapped at the sight of her looking wide-eyed and innocent.

"Well?" demanded Mrs. Smith, whose green eyes grew chilly at the sight of Elizabeth.

"Oh my, Mrs. Smith, are you stressed?" asked Elizabeth, concern in her voice. "Please Mrs. Smith, I can help you out with that."

"What did you say?" I asked slowly, deliberately.

Elizabeth swallowed. "Um, stress relief. It's part of my job."

Mrs. Smith's eyes were very green, staring at her with an intensity that startled her. Elizabeth felt her limited confidence starting to slip away. Perhaps she should leave her to it.

Don't be stupid Elizabeth, she told herself. If you do that, you'll be out of a job, there's barely any work for you as it is.

Without waiting for her stunning boss to say anything further Elizabeth stepped forward, quickly closing the gap between them. She reached out and gently pried her boss' hand off her pussy and covered it with her soft hand.

"Ah!" When her cool hand slid into my panties and her fingers touched my clit, I let out a small gasp of delight.

She rubbed it tenderly and then began to move her hand, sliding it up and down over my pussy.

I stared down as Elizabeth began to slowly rub my pussy with her soft hand.

Elizabeth wasn't quite sure if the look on her

boss' face was amazement or horror, but she was very fascinated by the sight of her small hand sliding up and down inside her panties. The busty blonde took the fact that she hadn't stopped her as an encouragement to carry on.

"That's it Mrs. Smith, let me take care of this for you," said Elizabeth encouragingly, hoping that she wouldn't suddenly order her to stop.

I managed to say, a bit of steel in my voice, "You aren't getting off that easily, honey. You've caused me too much stress for that."

Before Mrs. Smith's words had time to register in Elizabeth's mind, she found herself with her back on the desk, and her right leg flung over her boss' left shoulder.

"Now, my dear. I am going to grind my pussy into yours and keep doing it until I am completely relieved of the stress you have caused me."

With that, she dug into the V of Elizabeth's top and brought out her magnificent boobs, twisting the nipples and kneading tits like dough. Then she began to grind her pussy into Elizabeth's, as she mounted her on the desk.

I was in heaven. It was about fucking time, fuck being the operative word.

I stuck my finger in her mouth and commanded her to suck it. I imagined what it would feel like to grow a dick and fuck this girl. Would it feel as good?

I wanted everything at once and I wanted to punish her for the torture I had endured.

Mrs. Smith suddenly abandoned Elizabeth's leg and pussy,  and sat on her face instead. Elizabeth could barely breathe. So intensely did Mrs. Smith grind her pussy into her face, rubbing it up and down all over her face, not caring whether she smeared her makeup or not.

"If you want to keep your job, stick your tongue in that pussy and lick it like your life relies on it. I'm going to use your whole body for stress relief today. That will teach you to take your job a lot more seriously next time."

I was wild with desire like someone possessed. I rode her face hard, letting her breathe from time to time. But I wouldn't let myself come yet. I wanted everything. Who knew how much time I had before that lucky old whore, Esther Madison resumed?

"Fuck me. That's right, baby, fuck me!"

I heard some muffled responses from Elizabeth but who cares? All I could think was, Eat that pussy, bitch.

Then I thought, I wanted us to be naked and rubbing tits together. Abruptly I got up, locked the door, then turned around and faced Elizabeth as she rose from the desk with a startled almost frightened look on her wet messed face.

"But Mrs. Smith, what about Mr. Collins?"

Damn. Damn him to hell!

"Very well then. I guess you'll have to finish your job. Kneel."

She did exactly as she was told. Grabbing her by the back of the head, I stuffed her face in my pussy, turning her face into my fuck toy, telling myself I deserved satisfaction after all I had suffered at her hands.

I had a tremendous orgasm with my fist stuffed in my mouth to keep myself quiet. After all, Mr. Collins could be there at any moment.

Mrs. Smith was breathing heavily, staring at Elizabeth's face as her orgasm began to gradually wane. "Oh, your face, I..."

"Shhh," Elizabeth silenced her. "Don't worry about it. I'm happy to be of service. It's my job to help relieve your stress. I'll clean myself up no problem."

"Oh," Mrs. Smith said, still striving to catch her breath. "Thank you, Elizabeth."

The busty blonde gave Mrs. Smith's pussy one last affectionate nuzzle and then she got up. The slightly hairy entrance to her boss' pussy was still sticky with her juices. "Would you like me to..." she gestured at her boss' messy crotch and licked her upper lip with the tip of her tongue.

"No, you go get cleaned up," said Mrs. Smith curtly.

Her expression had suddenly gone from post-orgasmic bliss to poker face and Elizabeth wondered if she'd done something wrong. She was sure her boss had enjoyed that poon job. What had upset her?

"Okay Mrs. Smith," she said, leaving her boss to clean herself up. She was careful to peek around the door cautiously before closing it behind her.

The buxom secretary went to the bathroom and cleaned herself up as best she could, reapplying her makeup afterward. She wondered if her boss was angry or upset with her. After all, she'd offered to lick her pussy clean and she'd refused. At least, she believed that was what had happened.

As Elizabeth stepped back into the reception area of their offices she saw none other than Mr. Collins standing there waiting. Elizabeth started at the sight of him. How long had he been waiting there?

"Oh, Mr. Collins, welcome," Elizabeth greeted him as she quickly regained her composure.

Mr. Collins, the company's regional manager, was a well-dressed man in his mid-fifties. He still had a full head of hair, although it was almost pure snowy white, and his stern face was lined with deep wrinkles.

"You must be Elizabeth. I believe Mrs. Smith is expecting me," his voice was soft, almost a whisper, although it had a slightly sinister edge to it.

Elizabeth swallowed nervously. Hopefully, Mrs. Smith had finished straightening herself up in there.

"Yes, of course, Mr. Collins. Pass directly through." Elizabeth felt compelled to bow or curtsy for some reason, but she was able to hold it back as she moved aside and unlocked the door for Mr. Collins. He swept past her and into Mrs. Smith's office and Elizabeth breathed a small sigh of relief.

Hopefully, the meeting went well, Elizabeth was finally starting to make a breakthrough with Mrs. Smith, she hoped, and if her boss' meeting with Mr. Collins went well then her boss was sure to be in a good mood that afternoon.

# Chapter Six

## Another Encounter

Mrs. Smith's meeting with Mr. Collins lasted well into the afternoon and he eventually departed at about quarter to four. Mrs. Smith did seem pleased, or at the very least relieved, when she finally bid farewell to Mr. Collins.

Mrs. Smith stepped back into the office with a huge grin on her face. "Mr. Collins is over the moon!" she announced happily.

"That's wonderful!" said Elizabeth, standing up excitedly.

"And I was on fire in there! I've never felt so relaxed and at ease, thank you Elizabeth, you're the best personal assistant I've ever had!"

"Oh, thank you Mrs. Smith!" said Elizabeth

in delight. She hugged Mrs. Smith warmly, so happy to receive her praise.

"Oh, Elizabeth," I said in surprise as the gorgeous young blonde hugged me happily.

I stiffly put my arms around Elizabeth's waist as she pressed her lush curves up against me, my hands resting on the small of her back.

Elizabeth relaxed her embrace and made to step back, but my arms stiffly held her in place.

Mrs. Smith didn't say anything, but Elizabeth could feel her boss' heavy breathing in her ear.

"Oh, Elizabeth," repeated Mrs. Smith in a whisper.

My hands slid down from her back to cup and squeeze her ass through her black skirt, the firm spheres of her buttocks filling my palms.

Elizabeth froze, not sure what to do.

Both my hands were on her ass, squeezing and kneading, keeping her body held tightly against mine.

"Um... are you okay Mrs. Smith?" Elizabeth said eventually.

"How much longer are you going to tease me, Elizabeth?" I responded, releasing my young helper and moving backward away from her, "You're asking for problems. I've got to get going."

With that I headed back into my office, slamming shut the door behind me.

Elizabeth sighed in dismay. She was still unsure of her position with her odd, socially awkward superior.

# Chapter Seven

## Elizabeth is Determined

A determined Elizabeth arrived the next morning eager to please as always.

She had made sure to dress in the sexiest and most enticing garment she could find in her wardrobe, a clinging red mini-dress that hugged her ample curves and left little room for interpretation. It was particularly tight across the peachy globes of her firm buttocks.

Again Elizabeth dropped a pen on her way out of her boss' office and bent at the waist to retrieve it.

"Come here, Elizabeth," said Mrs. Smith in a soft voice that had a threatening quality to it.

Elizabeth did as she was told, wondering if

Mrs. Smith was annoyed. Or something else.

"Bend over the desk Elizabeth."

The buxom blonde nodded, following her boss's instructions and bending over the edge of her desk.

"Good job Elizabeth."

Elizabeth gasped as she felt both of Mrs. Smith's hands on her ass, squeezing her firm, toned buttocks.

"Oh my," breathed Mrs. Smith. "It's been too long, you're right."

After a moment of silence, Elizabeth looked back over her shoulder. "Are you okay Mrs. Smith?"

Mrs. Smith whimpered as she grabbed Elizabeth's naked ass with both hands and squeezed, her fingers sinking into the firm flesh of her round buttocks.

Mrs. Smith sighed as she kneaded the toned flesh of her blonde assistant's ass.

Elizabeth tensed slightly as she felt her move closer, her naked crotch sliding over one soft cheek of her ass.

"Good job Elizabeth," I repeated, leaning in against Elizabeth, my naked crotch sliding up along the crack of her ass and nestling between her glorious buttocks as I rubbed myself against her.

My hands slipped up off her ass to hold her by the hips and pull her ass back against my crotch.

"It is a shame I can't use my mouth to relieve you today. I don't want my husband complaining about my breath" said Elizabeth as her boss humped against her ass, her skirt bunched up against her waist.

Mrs. Smith gave a small moan as Elizabeth

turned round, rising from the desk. Then she began to rub her crotch against that of Mrs. Smith's.

They both moaned as they held on to one another, their tits hardening and rubbing against each other.

Elizabeth slipped a finger between her boss' legs, rubbing the tip of it against the lips of her boss' pussy.

"If you want this you can't keep hiding in your office and avoiding me all the time," warned Elizabeth.

"Yes," I moaned, my knees bent, my hands gripping Elizabeth's ass as I rode her finger. "Anything, whatever you want."

"And you have to tell me I'm doing a good job more often," added Elizabeth, determined to put an end to the awkwardness between them. Her boss was leaning in against her, Elizabeth's hand, the finger deep in her pussy.

"Absolutely," Mrs. Smith hurriedly agreed. She pushed forward with her hips as Elizabeth dropped her hand away.

Then her boss' finger slid smoothly into her wet pussy.

Elizabeth let out a loud moan as her temporary boss pushed two of her fingers inside her, rubbing her clit with her thumb. Her entry felt like the walls between them breaking down.

Mrs. Smith held tightly onto Elizabeth's ass with her other hand and thrust into her busty secretary's vagina several times and then pulled out.

"Wh...what's wrong?" asked Elizabeth, opening her eyes to look at Mrs. Smith. She wasn't going to go all cold on her again surely?

"That's not the hole I want. Not yet. We want to keep that mouth fresh for your husband, right?" Mrs. Smith calmly told her. Then without warning, she crushed her lips against Elizabeth's, kissing her violently.

Elizabeth mumbled in surprise as she felt her boss' tongue dueling with hers, felt her body rubbing against hers, her hands kneading her ass.

Elizabeth suddenly pushed her head back, stammering "I'm not sure...oh!" She gasped as Mrs. Smith suddenly pulled out her tits and sucked on a taut nipple hard. "Oh Mrs. Smith!"

I lavished attention on her beautiful boobs, licking, sucking, and slobbering like a hungry dog. My clit throbbed with need. But I also wanted her to enjoy herself.

"Turn around and bend over the desk," I instructed.

She did and I stood, bent over her and pushing my wet pussy into her ass as I bent over her back, rubbing my tits into her back as I softly moved her hair to the left side of her face- I gently kissed her neck and brought the kisses down her back.

As I reached her ass with my kisses I pulled her chair towards me and sat in it, bending in to kiss her beautiful ass. I squeezed my knees in between hers before forcing her knees apart.

I scooted my chair in closer to spread her legs and got a wonderful view of her ass and her wet pussy as my fingers gently ran circles from the back of her knees up her thighs, down to her knees, up the inside of her thighs as I gently kissed her butt cheeks and licked the crevice where her legs met her ass.

"Oh, Mrs. Smith," Elizabeth panted, "that feels so good." I kept kissing her butt cheeks. Then I ran my tongue down her crack to her asshole and flicked it with my wet tongue.

"Oh!" Elizabeth jumped. I was getting more and more aroused by the minute as I flattened my tongue against her pussy lips and licked upward to her asshole. As I kissed her asshole, pushing my tongue into her ass like I had kissed her lips, she moaned.

As I licked her pussy lips, poked my tongue slightly into her cunt, and continued licking up to her asshole, my hands continued to tickle the backs of her legs. She was panting, and as I inserted my tongue, I felt her asshole quiver.

I was licking up her lips to her hole for the

umpteenth time when she began spasming and pushing her ass against my face. "Aw fuck, that feels so good, I'm coming, Mrs. Smith, I'm coming all over your face!"

Her body shook and spasmed as I drove my tongue up her ass; at the time, I hadn't yet realized how much I liked fucking women with my tongue.

"Turn around and allow me to lick your clit, dear."

I reached her face with my hands and kissed her deep and strong on the lips, sucking her tongue and swirling mine in her mouth.

"Lie back on the desk and spread your legs," I demanded.

Elizabeth did and I had a wonderful view of her entire pussy. It was completely shaved and smooth-and her lips were wet and gleaming.

"I'm sucking this pussy till you come so many times you can't remember how many," I muttered as I leaned in.

She thrust her bare pussy into my face and exclaimed, "Oh, yes, Mrs. Smith!" as she opened her legs wide in the air.

I carefully avoided touching her clit as I ran my tongue up one side of her cunt and down the other, before sliding it up her slit because it was so moist. I could feel the cream from my pussy sliding down my crack into the office chair as I licked the flowing juices from her cunt.

"Oh, Mrs. Smith, your tongue feels SO good on my pussy. Lick my clit, Honey. I want to cover your lovely face with my cum."

Her words made me so horny; I was creaming in my chair with my fingers pushing steadily in my cunt as my face was creamed by her pussy; my tongue pushed so far up her cunt she was sitting on it at the edge of my desk as she was grabbing my hair and pushing her pussy into my face.

My cheeks were wet from her juice when I pushed my tongue as far as it would go. I then pulled my tongue out and sucked on her clitter, just as I had done with her nipples earlier.

I could feel her spasm against my mouth as she came. I was sucking every bit of her pussy and sticking my tongue as deep up her cunt as it would go.

She knelt to kiss me on the mouth after her spasms subsided, tasting her juice on my lips and tongue.

"You make me come so good, Mrs. Smith. Fuck, I love your tongue! But I know you'll be feeling stressed right now and I'd like to help you relieve your stress. Being your 'assistant', I guess I should make you 'feel good' on command."

She then slid off the desk, positioned herself between my knees, and gently lifted my knees toward my breasts, giving her a clear view of my pussy, while my legs were still resting on the arms of my office chair. She climbed up to kiss me on the lips and gently inserted her tongue into my mouth while rubbing her breasts up my pussy, stomach, and breasts.

"I've wanted your tongue in my pussy and wanted to lick yours since our first meeting," Elizabeth breathed into my ear as her hand played with my nipple.

"You made me nervous. I was drawn to you right away. Since then, I haven't had a single other thought," I whispered as she pushed her tits into my wide-open pussy with my legs crossed over the arms of my office chair. Then I saw her tongue run down to suck my nipple.

She trailed kisses down my stomach until her face reached my wide-open pussy. She leaned back and looked at me, licked her lips before bending in and licking my pussy lips with a very wet tongue. The sensation was overwhelming!

My husband did lick my pussy from time to time, but he was generally too worked up for him to spend much time doing it.

I felt it start to build and began to shake as my cunt spasmed into her face and pulled her beautiful blonde hair around my thighs and thrust my pussy toward her lips as she lapped up all of my juices and continued to lap until I could take no more.

In the aftermath, I pulled her up to kiss her lips, still tasting of my pussy, and hauled her lovely ass onto my lap as I stretched out to caress her breasts. I was glowing from head to toe.

"Good job Elizabeth. You may have awakened something bigger than you can handle" I whispered into her ear as I continued to play with her nipples.

# Chapter Eight

## Elizabeth is Happy

The rest of that day went like a dream for Elizabeth. For once Mrs. Smith didn't lock herself in her office, and she frequently came out to see Elizabeth, chatting breezily and regularly complimenting her on her work. Mrs. Smith was like an entirely different person.

When five o'clock came and Mrs. Smith was on her way home, she paused at Elizabeth's desk to say goodnight, insisting that she bend over so she could pat Elizabeth for a good job.

Mrs. Smith pulled up Elizabeth's skirt and ran her hands all over the smooth cheeks of her buttocks.

Elizabeth gasped as she felt her boss' tongue slide over the curve of her right cheek and gave her left buttock a tender kiss.

"I look forward to working with you tomorrow Elizabeth," she said in a husky whisper before slapping her on her exposed posterior and heading out the door.

Elizabeth sighed in contentment. She was certain that her job was now secure.

## Chapter Nine

### Guess Who?

The next day at work, Elizabeth arrived with a new sense of purpose. She was wearing a short black skirt and a matching black satin blouse. To impress Mrs. Smith, she'd carefully selected her underwear -- no bra and no panties to allow her easy access to her ass.

Elizabeth's thoughts were interrupted as she was startled by a pair of hands closing over her breasts, squeezing them firmly through her satin blouse.

"Oh! Good morning Mrs. Smith," she stammered in surprise as the hands boldly kneaded her ample hooters.

"Still not wearing a bra, are we?" came an unexpected, but familiar voice. Mrs. Madison was back!

# THE END

\-   **Maureen Lester**

www.ingramcontent.com/pod-product-compliance
Lightning Source LLC
Chambersburg PA
CBHW051453150726
48000CB00005B/2379